The Go-Away Doll

A Dr. H Book™

Written by Carl A. Hammerschlag, M.D.

Illustrated by Beverly E. Soasey

A TIPI Book For Kids

A Dr. H Book ™

The Dr. H imprint is a trademark of Turtle Island Press, Inc. (TIPI)

Published by Turtle Island Press, Inc.
3104 E. Camelback Road, Suite 614, Phoenix, Arizona 85016

http://www.turtleislandpress.com

Book design and illustration by Beverly E. Soasey

First edition: June 1998

Hardcover edition ISBN: 1-889166-22-7

Publisher's Cataloging-in-Publication
(Provided by Quality Books, Inc.)

Hammerschlag, Carl A.
     The go-away doll: A Dr. H book/written by Carl A.
Hammerschlag; illustrated by Beverly Soasey.--1st ed.
     p. cm.
     Preassigned LCCN: 97-62553
     ISBN: 1-889166-22-7 (hardcover): $16.95
     SUMMARY: Six year-old Cara loses her beloved doll, Monica,
while playing in the park. Her neighbor, Mr. Sidney, overhears
her sobbing, and begins to share with her the letters which
Monica sends him from her travels around the world.

     1. Dolls–Juvenile fiction. 2. Voyages and travels–
Juvenile fiction. 3. Loss (Psychology)--Juvenile fiction.
I. Soasey, Beverly. II. Title. III. Title: Go away doll

PZ7.H36 1998   813'.54 [E]
                               QBI98-120

10 9 8 7 6 5 4 3 2 1

Printed by: C & C Offset Printing Co., Ltd.
Hong Kong

Printed on recycled paper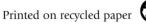

For Kyah, my sugar baby.
CAH

For my sons, Luke and Mark.
BES

TIPI is dedicated to publishing and marketing creative products
that enhance personal and community well-being.
We intend to inspire, teach principles of quality character and
contribute to charitable causes that preserve our natural resources.

TIPI

I looked at the bench next to the swings.

"Where's Monica? Mommy, where is she? I left her right there. Now she's gone!"

"I'll help you look for her, Cara. I know how much you love her."

Mommy hugged me and kissed me, and I started to cry.
"If we can't find her, I promise I'll buy you another doll."

Mommy was still holding me, and I was trying hard to stop crying.
I looked up over her shoulder, and there was our friend Mr. Sidney standing
in front of me. He lives in my apartment house on the floor above me.

"Hello, Cara. I just happened to be sitting on my favorite bench and I couldn't help overhearing what happened. Before Monica left, she gave me this note. It's for you. Do you want me to read it to you?"

"You talked to my Monica?" I asked Mr. Sidney.
"Really? How come she talked to you?"

"I don't know. I guess she trusted me. Monica said she thought I'd understand
how hard it can be to say goodbye to someone you love."

I stopped crying. "What does the note say, Mr. Sidney?"

He took out a piece of paper from his pocket and read it to me.

"To Cara, My Dearest Friend in the World, I have loved living with you in our room
and playing with you, but I have to go away for awhile. I want to see more
of the world. I may come back some day. In the meantime, I will send Mr. Sidney
messages about my travels and he will tell you where I am. I love you, Monica."

"Will you, Mr. Sidney? Will you let me know when you hear from Monica?"

"I'd be delighted to pass on Monica's messages. It sounds as if she plans to do quite a bit of traveling. I'll look for you here in the park, Cara. I come here often."

When I saw him again, I got so excited. Mr. Sidney was waving a postcard in the air.

"It comes from Arizona." Mr. Sidney showed me a card of a girl, maybe a little older than me, sitting on a horse. She had black hair that hung down past her shoulders.

"Look at her belt."

"Yes, it's beaded. Her skirt and blouse are made of deerskin. The horse has no saddle because that's how they ride—bareback."

Mr. Sidney read the card.

Cara, my sister,
This Apache girl calls me Shidizhe, "little Sister." Here, in this magical place I have learned that all people are sisters and brothers, and all the other creatures, too: Rabbit, Eagle, Coyote, the Owl, and newborn Lamb.

In her village the Grandfathers and Grandmothers teach the children about the plants they can eat and which ones they can use for medicine and about ways and spirits. My Shidizhe is learning to do beadwork. The lightning bolts stand for life, among her people. It is very exciting to ride on horseback!

Your Best Friend,
Monica

ARIZONA 30

APACHE 20

To Cara
c/o Mr. Sidney

"I wish I could be there, too."

"Do you know about the Apache, Cara?"

I shook my head no.

"Well, I found this library book and brought it with me."

Mr. Sidney showed me the Arizona desert and mountains where the Apache live. They once lived in houses called wikiups and were fierce warriors. They believe all the creatures on the earth are our relatives.

That night I put the postcard on my pillow—the one I used to share with Monica—
and I had a dream. I met Sister Owl and Brother Coyote and even littlest Sister Squirrel.
They were all nestled together in a cave.

In the morning I felt as if I had been with Monica.

The next time I saw Mr. Sidney he had heard from Monica, from Africa.
The dark-skinned girl in the picture was squinting in the bright sunlight.
Her black hair was braided. She wore many strands of necklaces around her neck.
She was standing in the doorway of her house. The outside walls were painted in
brightly colored patterns.

Mr. Sidney read
the card to me.

Jambo Cara,

My fried Taz lives in Zimbabwe, Africa.
She is Zulu. This is her home. It's called
a kraal. Taz's father is a gamekeeper.
I went with her into the jungle. I saw
elephants. They are so huge. They look
like mountains walking! When the lions
roar, everything else gets still.

Love,
Monica

To Cara
c/o Mr. Sidney

ZULU
ZIMBABWE
AFRICA

Zebra
AFRICA

AFRICA 199

I held the postcard and looked at the picture while Mr. Sidney told my mom about a show at the museum on the tribes of Africa.

"Maybe we could take a walk there one afternoon," Mom said. "Mr. Sidney says there is an exhibit on the Zulu."

"Let's go, Mom!"

I added the postcard to the other one on my pillow that night. I dreamt I was playing with lion cubs. Playful elephants showered me with cool water and mud.
When I got up, I told my stuffed animals, "I sure hope Monica comes back.
I'm going to tell her I was with her everywhere she was."

The next postcard came from Sweden. It showed a girl wearing a long white robe.
On her head she had a wreath of evergreens with candles burning in it.

Mr. Sidney read,

Hej, Cara,

The sun has barely come up today. It only glows on the horizon for a short time. The candles that my friend Karin wears are for Santa Lucia Day. This day is a celebration of lights in the darkest part of winter. The candles remind people of the coming light. I ate too many sweet rolls though, and got a little sick.

Love you,
Monica

To Cara
c/o Mr. Sidney

"I love her candle crown, and look, she's wearing wooden shoes."

"Yes, she is. Would you like to wear a crown like Karin's?"

"Oh, yes."

Mr. Sidney showed me how to make a crown out of twigs.
Then we stuck little branches into it to make pretend candles.
When I put it on, I looked just like Karin.

"Do you think Monica will ever come back home to me, Mr. Sidney?"

"I know you'd like for her to come back, but Monica has learned that there
are many places to call home."

Next, Mr. Sidney brought me a card from Japan. On this postcard a little boy held a fishing net with a huge fish in it. He wore a short, quilted blue and white coat and loose pants. His black hair was cut short and he had a big smile.

He read the postcard to me.

"Mr. Sidney, she's coming back. Monica's coming back!
When is she coming?
Tell me. Do you know?"

Mr. Sidney just smiled and shrugged.

Ikaga Desuka, Cara,

Taku is my friend. He lives in Sakata, Japan. The salmon he holds feeds his whole family. His family makes furniture and wood carvings which are so beautiful. I hope to bring one home for you soon.

Love,
Monica

To Cara
c/o Mr. Sidney

That night I set Taku's picture with the others and dreamed that Monica was riding
on the back of a fat, silvery salmon. He was in the ocean trying to decide which river was
the way home. I was waving to Monica, but she couldn't see me. The salmon
winked at me though!

In the morning I remembered my dream. I just knew Monica would be home soon.

I took my cards to school for "show and tell" and I told the kids about all the
different places and people on them. I said that my doll was going to come back.

Two boys laughed at me. "She'll never come back, you're just making it up" one of them
said. "You'll never see your Go-Away Doll again."

That's what he called her, "Go-Away Doll," but he was wrong.
I knew he was.

When I ran up to Mr. Sidney next time, he was sitting on his favorite bench. He was smiling. When I got close, his smile got bigger.

"Do you have another card? I asked. "Where is it?"

Mr. Sidney moved over and patted the bench next to him, and then I saw he was hiding something.

"What do you have?"

"A surprise, Cara. For you." He pulled out a doll. She was dressed in a quilted coat with a beaded belt. She wore wooden clogs and in her hand was a small wooden turtle.

"That's not my Monica, Mr. Sidney."

"She does look different doesn't she? We probably look different to her too. She has been gone for quite awhile. Monica has traveled so far and made so many new friends. She has even shared her incredible experiences."

I picked her up and felt the soft quilting, touched the beaded belt and soft deerskin dress. "She is very beautiful, my Monica." I kissed and hugged her and jumped up and down with Mr. Sidney.

Then I noticed a gold locket around Monica's neck.

"What's this?"

"This is something special from me to you because I have to go away now, but my heart will always be with you."

"Will you come back Mr. Sidney?"

"I believe I will."

"Just like Monica," I said, as I danced with Mr. Sidney.

When it was time to leave, I gave Mr. Sidney a big hug and we said goodbye.

I'm going to miss him.

Pronunciation Guide

Shidizhe.............................shi-DAY-dzuh

Zimbabwe...........................zim-BOB-way

Kraal...................................krahl

Hej......................................hay

Santa Lucia.......................santa lu-SEE-ah

Wikiup................................WICKEY-up

Ikaga Desuka.....ee-KAH-gah DAY-sue-kah

Sakata..................................sa-KAH-ta

Acknowledgments

These are some of the people who have shared responsibility for this creative venture. Lisa Cohen first suggested my stories be written for children. Juanita Havill, a talented writer of children's books herself, became my editorial consultant and mentor. Kyle Porter read my first story, frowned, and reminded me to stop rambling. Tara Sues packaged, printed, and produced this book, without her it could not have happened. Beverly Soasey's illustrations and presence have supported every step, and Barbara Pikus finalized the caricatured imprint for Dr. H Books. My grandchildren have listened to The Go Away Doll's many incarnations and raised important questions I had not previously considered. And to Charlie Clark, Natalie Lang, Mary Jo Godwin, Dennis Kirk, among many others who have helped through this process—my heartfelt thanks.

CAH